CW00794443

Usborne

A Sticker Dolly Story
Little Lost Deer

Zanna Davidson

Illustrated by Katie Wood
Cover illustration by Antonia Miller

Use the stickers to dress the Dolls on the 'Meet the Dolls' pages

Meet the
Animal Rescue Dolls

Zoe, Amelia and Jack are the 'Animal Rescue Dolls'. They look after the animals that live on the Wild Isle, helping animals in trouble and caring for any that are injured.

Jack

has a passion for sea creatures. He is also a keen birdwatcher and is never without his binoculars.

Use the stickers to dress the Dolls

Zoe

is brilliant at working with wild horses and loves riding. She is also fascinated by reptiles.

Amelia

has a special bond with dogs and rabbits. She also adores having pets of her own.

Dolly Town

The Animal Rescue Dolls work at the Animal Sanctuary, in
Dolly Town, home to all the Dolls. The Dolls work in teams to help
those in trouble and are the very best at what they do, whether
that's animal rescue, magical missions or protecting the planet.
Each day brings with it an exciting new adventure...

The **Shooting Star** train
whisks the Dolls away
on their missions.

Madame Coco's
Costume Emporium
has everything the
Dolls might need.

The Dolls love to
celebrate at the
Cupcake Café.

Rose Theatre

The **Animal Sanctuary** is where
the Animal Rescue Dolls work.

Bluebell Bookshop

**Evergreen
Sports
Arena**

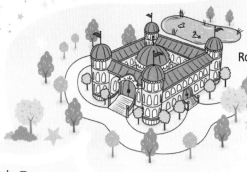
Royal Palace

Palm Tree
Film Studios

Fashion Design
Studio

HEARTBEAT

Heartbeat
Dance Academy

Mission Control Centre
lets the Dolls know
who's in trouble and
where to go.

Pop Star
Stadium

Silver Sparkles
Skating Rink

Strawberry
Lane Stables

Honeysuckle Cottage

Chapter One

Wild
Fire

It was a gorgeous sunny afternoon and the Animal Rescue Dolls, Jack and Zoe, were busy in the Animal Sanctuary.

"Oh look, Jack!" said Zoe, pointing at the window. "Isn't that your crow?"

Jack turned to see his crow,

hopping about on the windowsill, pecking at the glass to be let in. Jack laughed and went over to the window. He'd helped to mend the crow's wing, but even after releasing him into the wild, the crow kept coming back to the sanctuary to say hello. Jack couldn't resist offering him some seeds.

"And how's
your baby turtle?"
Jack asked Zoe,
as the crow flew
off, satisfied with
his treat.

Zoe's face broke into a smile.
"She's adorable! She was in such
a sorry state when we found her,
but she just needs to gain a little
more weight and she'll be ready
for release."

Just then, the door swung open
and Amelia came into the sanctuary.

At once, Alfie, her pet rescue dog, bounded up to her, barking with excitement.

"I've had such a good day," she told the others, bending down to greet Alfie. "I re-homed the tabby cat and the new owners were so happy to have her. They had lots of toys ready for her, too."

Tigerlily – RE-HOMED

"That's brilliant news," said Jack. "It's such a relief when we can find new homes for our rescue animals."

Before he could say anything else, all the Dolls' watches began to flash.

Zoe hurried over to the table and picked up her olive green tablet, tapping on the flashing paw print.

"Mission Control here!" came a voice. "Are the Animal Rescue Dolls there?"

"Yes, we're all here," said Zoe.

"What's happening?"

"I'm afraid there's trouble on the Wild Isle. A fire has spread through the Emerald Forest."

Don't worry! The fire has gone out now, and no animals were harmed, but a mother deer has been seen, wandering the forest without any sign of her fawn. We think she could have been separated from her mother in the fire and become lost. The fawn would only be about a week old and she needs her mother's milk.

"The poor little fawn," said
Amelia. "I do hope she's okay.
She must have been so worried
by the fire. Of course we'll help."

"We'll do everything we can to
find the fawn," added Jack.

"We'll send through the mission
details now," said Mission Control.

MISSION LOCATION:
The Wild Isle

Dragonfly
Wetlands

Misty
Marshes

MISSION INFORMATION:

A baby fallow deer has
been separated from her
mother after a fire.

She is only about a week old.
Baby fallow deer can stand
within 10 minutes of being born,
and walk within a few hours.

She will be in need of
milk and warmth.

It's important to find the baby
deer before nightfall as she will
be much safer with the herd.

THE LITTLE LOST DEER:

Large ears

Large
dark eyes

Speckled coat
with white spots

Black and
white tail

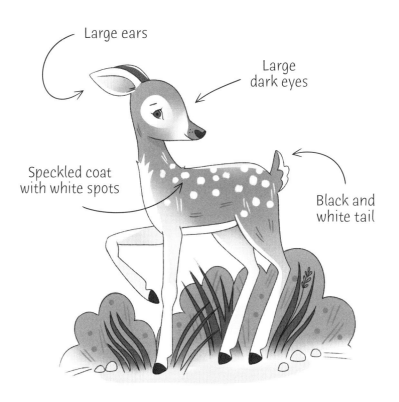

A baby deer is called a fawn.

"Thank you!" said Zoe. "We'll be there as soon as we can. It's Mission Go!"

Chapter Two

A Magic Whistle

The Dolls began hurrying around the Animal Sanctuary, making sure all the animals had enough food and water before they left.

"We should take milk for the baby deer," said Jack, heading to the store cupboard. "If she hasn't fed for a while, we'll need to give her milk as soon as we find her."

"But we don't have any deer milk," said Amelia, anxiously.

"That's okay," Jack replied. "Goat milk will do and luckily we have some in stock. I'll make up a couple of bottles, just to be on the safe side, and I'll put them in my special bottle bag to keep warm."

As Jack made up the milk he turned to the others. "The hardest part is going to be finding the fawn. Mother deer hide their fawns in long grass, and only visit them every few hours or so. A tiny fawn…in such a huge area… It's going to be really tricky."

Amelia's face lit up. "Why don't we bring Alfie? I can keep him on his lead, so he won't scare the fawn, but he might help us to find her?"

"That's a great idea," said Zoe.

"Come on then, Alfie," said Amelia, turning to her dog. "Are you ready for your first mission?"

Alfie gave a bark, and Amelia clipped on his lead. Then together, they all stepped out into the sunshine.

"First stop, Madame Coco's Costume Emporium!" said Zoe. "She's sure to have everything we'll need."

As the Dolls walked across the street, they saw birds swooping through the sky. A breeze was stirring but the afternoon still held some of the warmth of the day.

"I always love coming here," said Zoe, when they reached Madame Coco's.

"And now Alfie gets to come too," added Jack, with a grin.

Together, they made their way through the revolving doors to the famous glass elevator.

"Hello, Jasper," said Amelia, smiling at the lift attendant. "Can you take us to the Animal Rescue Department? We're on an important mission."

It looks as if Alfie is excited about the mission too!

"Of course," said Jasper. "Step inside."

Jasper pressed the button and a moment later, they were all in the lift, gliding up and up before coming to a stop with a gentle

TING!

The Dolls stepped out into a
spacious room filled with all the
clothes they could need for every
kind of mission – from wetsuits for
underwater rescues to snowsuits
for misty mountains.

They looked up to see Madame
Coco coming towards them,
looking incredibly glamorous in a
long, silk dress.

"Oh no you don't, Alfie," said
Amelia, as Alfie tugged on his lead.

"Now, what can I do for you today?" Madame Coco asked.

"There's been a fire on the Wild Isle," explained Jack. "Luckily, no animals have been hurt, but a baby deer has been separated from her mother, and we must find her before nightfall."

"This is serious," said Madame Coco. "Now, let me think…what will you need?"

Even as she spoke, Madame Coco began whirling around the department floor, pulling out boots and blankets, trousers and jackets, with a stream of assistants running along behind her.

"Here you go," she said to the Animal Rescue Dolls, and she was smiling now. "I've found the perfect outfit for each of you, to help you on your mission."

Jack's clothes

A lightweight camouflage down jacket

A soft cotton T-shirt

Thick black lace-up boots

Grey canvas hiking trousers

Amelia's clothes

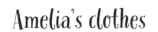

Cherry-red waterproof jacket

High-waisted stretch hiking trousers

Tan walking boots with extra grip

Padded no-pull luxury harness and lead for Alfie

Zoe's clothes

A magenta fleece-lined jacket with hood

Black waterproof softshell boots

Teal trekking leggings with pockets

"Thank you, Madame Coco," said Zoe. "These look brilliant."

"I do hope they're a good fit," said Madame Coco, ushering them towards the changing rooms.

The Dolls' names flashed up above the changing room doors and the Animal Rescue Dolls stepped inside. When they stepped out again…

41

"You'll need a first aid kit," said Madame Coco, "although I hope you don't have to use it. I've packed blankets for the baby deer as well, and here are two canvas rucksacks to carry everything."

"Thank you, Madame Coco,"
said Jack. "You think of everything."

"There's one more thing I want
to give you," added
Madame Coco, and
she handed over a
small, carved
piece of hollow
wood, flecked
with sparkling silver.

Jack took it, holding it carefully
in his hands. "Oh, it's a whistle!"
he said in surprise.

Madame Coco nodded. "When a

mother deer is looking for her fawn, she will call to it and the fawn will bleat in reply. If you blow through this whistle, it will make the sound of a mother deer," she explained. "With luck, the fawn will answer."

"Thank you," said Jack, slipping the whistle carefully into his jacket pocket.

Then the Dolls turned to go, Alfie trotting along behind them.

"Goodbye!" called Madame Coco. "And good luck!"

When the Dolls were out on the street once more, Jack tapped his watch to summon the Shooting Star train. In no time at all, it was whizzing towards them in a swirl of glittering dust.

"Where can I take
you today?" asked Sienna,
smiling at all the Dolls.

"To the Wild Isle, please,"
said Zoe. "We're searching for a
missing deer. The herd was last
seen at the edge of the Emerald
Forest and the Misty Marshes."

The doors glided to a close
behind them and then the
Shooting Star was off, winding its
way through Dolly Town until it
came to a dark tunnel, filled with
hundreds of tiny stars.

With a

WHOOSH

they shot out the other side.

The train skimmed over the
Misty Marshes of the Wild Isle
and the Dolls looked out, their
faces pressed against the window,
at the endless water, stretching
either side, dotted with beautiful
reed beds, wreathed in mist.

At the edge of the marshes, where the Emerald Forest once began, the train came to a halt and the Dolls – and Alfie – stepped outside.

All around them they could see blackened stumps where the trees had burnt to the ground,

and pieces of ash, still floating in the warm, still air.

They called their thanks to Sienna as she sped away, leaving them alone in the wild emptiness of the island.

Chapter Three
Darkness Falls

"I can't believe this much of the forest has gone," said Amelia. "The fire must have been so scary for the animals."

"Terrifying," added Jack, looking around. "It's almost unrecognisable, isn't it? Where do you think we should start looking?"

"Let's try the special whistle that Madame Coco gave us," suggested Zoe.

"Of course," said Jack. "Good idea!" He pulled it from his pocket and began to blow. At once, the whistle itself began to glow, and the air shimmered with tiny sparkles that

spread out across the forest.
Jack looked down at the whistle
in amazement. "There's definitely
something magical about this
whistle!" he said.

"Yes!" said Zoe. "I'm sure it
was made by the Magic Dolls."

"There's no answer though," said Jack, listening intently to the sounds of the forest. "The fawn must be some distance away. But where?"

"Let's think this through," said Amelia. "If the fawn was nearby, the mother would have been able to follow her scent. She's unlikely to be in the burnt part of the forest, as there's nowhere for her to hide. And the fawn hasn't answered our call. My guess is that she fled in the opposite direction to the herd."

Zoe nodded, her face thoughtful.

"I'll check the map," she said, pulling it up on her screen. "Okay, let's see…if the fawn fled in the opposite direction, that means she would have gone to the Dragonfly Wetlands, or the Misty Marshes."

"She can't be in the wetlands," said Jack, "not unless she swam across."

"But there's a bridge from the forest to the marshes," said Amelia. "Shall we try the Misty Marshes first?"

"Let's!" agreed Zoe. And the Dolls set off across the bridge, Alfie leading the way.

The further into the marshes they
went, the colder it grew. The mist
lay close to the ground, and all they
could hear was the soft squelch of
their footsteps in the mud, the hoot
of a heron and the low booming call
of a bittern. Jack kept calling on the
whistle, but there was no answer.

"Perhaps the fawn is hiding somewhere and is too scared to answer?" suggested Zoe.

"At least it's muddy here, so we should be able to spot any tracks," said Amelia, scanning the ground.

"The light's already dropping though," Jack noted, "and it's getting much harder to pick anything out."

He turned on his torch and
they all followed its beam,
searching for hoofprints.

"There!" Jack cried suddenly.
"Fallow deer tracks! I'm sure of it.
And look how small they are.
Only…that's odd," he added.

"What is it?" asked Amelia.

"I think there might be two sets
of tracks," said Jack, crouching
down to look more closely. "But
that doesn't make sense. And the
other pair look like they belong to
a fawn too."

As the dusk began to draw in, Jack blew on the whistle again, but this time the only answer came from the quiet croak of toads and the roosting calls of the water birds.

"Let's still follow the tracks," said Zoe. "They're our best lead yet."

They set off, deeper and deeper

into the marsh, following the trail.
Alfie had his nose to the ground
now, sniffing, his ears alert.

"Do you think he's picked up
a scent trail?" asked Zoe.

"I do hope so," said Amelia,
holding tight to his lead.

Then suddenly, as they arrived
at a thick bed of reeds, the tracks
came to an abrupt halt.

Alfie wagged his tail and tugged
harder at the lead.

"He's found something!" said
Amelia, excitedly.

"And just in time too," added
Jack. "The light is fading fast."

Amelia spoke to Alfie soothingly, keeping her voice calm. "Slow down now," she said, as he led her along a winding path through the reeds.

Alfie's nose was still to the ground, and his tail was wagging ever more frantically.

"We must be nearly there now," Amelia whispered back to the others.

Then came a loud beating of
wings and, in a flurry, two large
geese took off from the reed bed.

Alfie gazed up at their flight path. Looking around, the Dolls couldn't see any sign of the fawn in the nearby reeds.

"Alfie must have been following the scent of the geese," said Amelia, her voice full of dismay. "We still don't know if we're any closer to finding the fawn."

And then, in the distance, came a strange, haunting call, ringing out across the marsh.

"What's that?" asked Amelia.

"I think it's a lynx," Jack replied,

"a type of wild cat. They'll be starting to hunt around now."

"Oh no!" said Zoe. "That means the fawn is in real danger."

We have to find her, and fast.

Chapter Four

An
Answering Call

As they stood together in the gathering dark, Jack reached again for his whistle. Its silver sparkles lit the dusk and this time, to their great excitement, there was a little answering bleat.

"Did you hear that?" said Amelia, her eyes lighting up.

Jack nodded. "It didn't sound too far away!"

Alfie pricked up his ears again and wagged his tail.

"I think it was coming from that direction," said Zoe, pointing back the way they came.

Jack blew the whistle once more, and again came the faint reply.

"Now it sounds as if it's coming from over there," said Jack, pointing deeper into the marsh. "It's as if the answer is shifting in the wind."

Amelia bent down by Alfie's side. "Come on, Alfie," she said encouragingly. "Let's see if you can pick up the right scent trail this time."

Alfie wagged his tail and plunged into the reeds again, straining at his lead. Amelia went after him, with Jack and Zoe close behind, shining their torches to light the way.

"He's definitely onto something," said Amelia. "I just hope it's the fawn..."

"I think we're in luck!" cried
Jack. "Hold Alfie back."

For there, lit up in the darkness,
its eyes shining in the torchlight,
was a tiny baby fawn, huddled
among the reeds.

"Isn't she beautiful?" Jack whispered. "We need to be as quiet as we can. I don't want to startle her."

But the fawn didn't get up when she saw them. Instead, she just looked at them with wide, blinking eyes. Amelia coaxed Alfie away, so as not to alarm the fawn, while Jack approached as quietly as he could, a fluffy blanket at the ready.

Then Amelia crouched down next to Alfie.

"Well done, boy," she said, giving
him one of his favourite treats.
"You've done brilliantly today."

Zoe gave Alfie a pat, then looked
over to Jack. She didn't want to
come any closer in case she

overwhelmed the fawn, but she was longing to know how she was.

"Is she okay?" she asked, keeping her voice to a whisper. She knew Jack was an expert when it came to wild mammals.

"She's shivering," said Jack, as he gently placed the blanket over her. "I think with the cold. This should help too..."

As he spoke, he pulled a warm bottle of milk from his bag and gently placed the teat in the fawn's mouth.

At first, the fawn seemed unsure what to do, but Jack squeezed the bottle so she could taste the warm milk inside, and then she began to suck.

"Oh! Look at that!" said Zoe. "She must be hungry."

"And she's so gorgeous," added
Amelia, "those huge dark eyes and
her little spotted coat."

In what seemed like no time,
the fawn had finished the milk.
Jack reached down to pick her up,
still wrapped snugly in the blanket.

"Right," he said, gently, "let's
get you back to your mother." Then
he glanced over at the others.
"The less time we spend with the
fawn the better. We don't want
her to imprint on us."

"What's imprinting?" asked Amelia.

"If you spend too much time with a very young fawn, they can end up thinking you're the mother," Jack explained. "We don't want this one to reject her real mother. I wouldn't normally approach a fawn at all, unless I really knew it was in trouble. We have to make sure we don't leave our scent on the fawn either, as that can make the mother reject her baby."

But as they turned to go, Alfie kept straining at the lead, refusing to leave.

"That's strange," said Amelia.

"Maybe there's another bird in the reeds," suggested Zoe.

"But we must get back," said Jack. "I need to get this fawn to her mother right now. If we leave it too long, they might reject each other."

Amelia tried tugging the lead again, and calling Alfie's name, but he ignored her.

"You two go ahead and I'll catch up," she said. "I just want to find out what's bothering him."

"Okay," said Zoe. "Call us on our watches if you need us."

Amelia nodded, turned on her
torch and began to follow Alfie.
He seemed relieved she was letting
him strike his own path and led her
around a little mound. Seconds
later, Amelia was calling out to
Jack and Zoe.

"Quick! Come back!" she cried.
"You'll never believe what I've found!"

Chapter Five
A Hidden Surprise

At the sound of her call, Jack and Zoe hurried back to Amelia's side.

"In there!" said Amelia, pointing just ahead. "Can you see?"

Zoe gave a gasp. "Oh my goodness!" she said. "It's another fawn!"

"The mother deer must have had twins," said Jack. "It's unusual but it does happen!"

"And that explains those double tracks," added Zoe.

"Luckily, I've a bottle of milk and a blanket for this one, too," said Jack.

He carefully put the first fawn down on the ground, next to her twin. Then he put a blanket over the second fawn and reached for the other bottle in his bag.

"Could I feed this one?" asked
Zoe, gazing at the little creature
trembling in the torchlight. He
seemed so slender and fragile, she
was longing to help him.

"Of course," Jack whispered back.

"Here you go." He handed Zoe the bottle and she crouched down, keeping as much distance as she could and being careful not to make eye contact with the fawn, to make sure he wouldn't imprint on her.

She could soon feel him though, sucking on the bottle, and she felt a swell of warmth, knowing she was helping this beautiful animal.

As soon as the fawn had finished the milk, she gave back the bottle.

"How was that?" Jack asked.

"Magical!" Zoe replied, smiling.

Jack nodded, and then they
each picked up a fawn and began
walking back across the Misty
Marshes, Amelia leading the way.
By now, the stars were shining

brightly, and the marshes were
lit by the beautiful silvery glow
of the moon.

"Isn't this amazing," said Jack.
"Not one, but *two* rescued fawns.

I couldn't be happier."

"And it's all down to Alfie," said Zoe. "We'd never have known about the second fawn if he hadn't picked up on the scent."

"Even if he did lead us on a wild goose chase at first," said Amelia, laughing.

After they crossed the bridge into the Emerald Forest, they passed the blackened stumps until they reached the green growth of trees again.

"I don't know why," said Zoe,

"but I can't shake off the feeling that we're being watched."

"I feel the same way," said Amelia. "Isn't that strange?"

Jack, however, was busy looking around for signs of the herd. "According to the Mission Map," he said, "this is near to where the herd was last seen. Oh look!" he added, pointing his torch at the ground. "I can definitely see signs that the herd passed this way. Let's leave the fawns here, in this patch of undergrowth."

Jack and Zoe placed the two fawns together in the shelter of a low bush, and then stepped away. "We can watch over the fawns from a distance, until the mother comes," said Jack.

Hopefully it won't take her long to pick up on the scent.

They walked between the trees until they came to another clump of bushes. "We can hide here," said Jack. "We should be downwind of the herd, so we won't stop the mother from returning."

They crouched down and waited. Alfie was quiet too, as if he knew what was expected of him.

"Good boy," whispered Amelia, giving him a stroke. "You're doing so well on your first mission."

After just a few minutes, they heard a rustling up ahead, and a

deer stepped between the trees.
Bathed in moonlight, they could
see her ears were pricked, her
black nose sniffing the air.

"Oh!" said Zoe, smiling. "Do you think that's the mother?"

Jack switched his binoculars to night vision mode. "I'm sure of it," he said. "I can see from her udders that she's recently given birth."

"And she's definitely sensed her fawns," added Amelia, in an excited whisper.

The deer began to move
towards the fawns and they
all held their breath.

But then Jack, still clutching his binoculars, gave a gasp. "That strange feeling you both had…of being watched," he said. "I think I know why! There's a lynx in the bushes up ahead. She must have been following us. She's very near the fawns. And I think she's ready to pounce!"

Chapter Six

A Moonlit Ride

F or a moment, the Dolls were frozen to the spot, their eyes all fixed on the lynx.

Then everything happened so quickly. The mother deer sniffed the air again, and charged forward, barking in alarm. The lynx looked up at her through narrowed eyes… and fled, disappearing into the forest as silently as she came.

The Dolls watched as the
mother deer made her way over
to the fawns. She nuzzled them
and they rose up onto their little
legs to be near her.

"What a lovely moment to end our mission on," said Zoe, smiling as she watched them. "Isn't that wonderful to see?"

"It is," agreed Jack. "Aren't we lucky!"

As quietly as they could, they all turned and began walking back through the trees, to where the Emerald Forest ended and the Misty Marshes began.

When they reached the bridge, Amelia tapped her watch to call the Shooting Star.

Moments later, it sped into view. "Hello, Animal Rescue Dolls," said Sienna, as the train drew to a halt. "How was your mission?"

"A success," said Zoe, grinning.

"Not one, but two baby deer rescued," added Amelia.

"Now we'd like to celebrate at the Cupcake Café, please!" said Jack.

"Step aboard," said Sienna.

"But first," she suggested, "how would you feel about a moonlit ride over the Wild Isle? It's such a beautiful night."

"Oh, we'd love that," said Amelia. "Thank you!"

Sienna pulled the Shooting Star away slowly, drawing it up into the air in a gentle arc, until they were hovering above the Emerald Forest, lit silver by the moon.

"Oh! It's amazing to see the
Wild Isle like this," said Jack, as the
magical train rode still higher and
headed west, over the Frozen Lake,
shimmering and sparkling, reflecting
the star-studded sky above.

The train turned, arcing east

towards the Rugged Mountains, weaving its way between the jagged peaks.

Far below, beneath tumbling cliffs, they could see the shadowy sea foaming and crashing against the rocks.

Then the Shooting Star began following the path of the Great Fish River, running beside its glittering waters until they were back where they began.

The Dolls took one last look at the Wild Isle, bathed in moonlight, and then they were in the tunnel once more, heading back to Dolly Town.

WHOOSH!

"Thank you!" said Jack, as they pulled up outside the Cupcake Café. "That was truly magical!"

The Dolls all waved goodbye as they stepped off the train, smiling as they saw the café lit up for the evening, little candles flickering on each of the tables, glowing lights hanging in swathes from the ceiling.

"Hello, Animal Rescue Dolls," said Maya, the café owner, showing them to their favourite table. "What can I get you? Hot chocolates as usual?"

"Yes please," said Zoe. "With marshmallows and cream!"

When Maya came back from the kitchen, she had a tray piled high with treats. "I've brought a biscuit for Alfie, too," she said. "He looks exhausted!"

"He came on the mission with us," said Amelia proudly, "his very first. He helped us find two baby deer in the undergrowth. I'm not sure we could have done it without him."

"What an amazing adventure," said Maya.

"It was," agreed Zoe. "I can't wait for our next one."

Then the Dolls turned to each other, and chanted, "Animal Rescue Dolls forever!"

The End

Join the **Dolphin Rescue Dolls**
in an exciting summer adventure

Read on for a sneak peek…

O livia tapped her watch.
"Come in, Mission Control,"
she said. "The team is ready.
What's the mission?"

"Sorry to take you away from
the Summer Party, but we have an
EMERGENCY. We've had a call
from Princess Callista on Coral

Island. The princess has noticed a dolphin mother and her baby trapped in a bay – they're circling around and can't get out again. They seem lost and confused. The princess's parents are preparing for an important visit and she didn't know who else to ask for help."

Jack, Holly and Olivia exchanged glances and nodded.

"Of course we'll come and help," said Holly.

"Thank you," said Mission Control. "We needed a Princess Doll as it's happening in royal waters, and an Animal Rescue Doll

to help with the dolphin rescue.
We asked for a Magic Doll, too, in
case you need to ask the mermaids
for help. I know you've never
worked together before," Mission
Control went on, "but you'll make
the perfect team. We'll send
through the mission details now…"

The rescue mission and events in this book are entirely fictional and should never be attempted by anyone other than a trained professional.

Edited by Lesley Sims and Stephanie King
Designed by Hannah Cobley and Jacqui Clark
Additional design by Johanna Furst
Additional illustrations by Heather Burns
Expert advice from Suzanne Rogers

First published in 2022 by Usborne Publishing Ltd., Usborne House, 83-85 Saffron Hill, London EC1N 8RT, England. usborne.com Copyright © 2022 Usborne Publishing Ltd. UKE